ALLAN AHLBERG

Chickens in the Snow

Illustrated by
ANDRÉ AMSTUTZ

PUFFIN BOOKS
Published by the Penguin Group: London, New York, Australia, Canada and New Zealand
Penguin Books Ltd, Registered Offices: Harmondsworth, Middlesex, England

Published in Puffin Books 2001
1 3 5 7 9 10 8 6 4 2

Printed in Hong Kong by Imago Publishing Ltd

A CIP catalogue record for this book is available from the British Library

ISBN 0–140–56404–7

It is Christmas Eve.
Snow is falling on the Hen House.
The chickens are all excited.
"Santa is coming!"

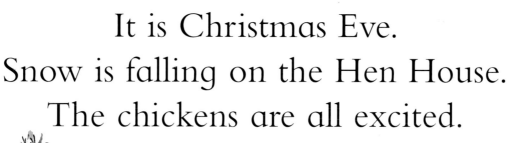

Out in the woods
Santa puts on
his big black boots.

After breakfast
Mother Hen makes a cake.
The chickens run around.
Slow Dog climbs up a ladder

. . . and falls off it.

Out in the woods
Santa puts on his long red coat.

In the afternoon
Mother Hen makes a jelly.
The chickens run around.
Slow Dog climbs on a chair

. . . and falls off it.

Out in the woods
Santa puts on his
soft white whiskers.

In the evening
Mother Hen puts the chickens to bed.
The chickens jump out of bed.
Mother Hen puts them
back in again.
And again.
And again.
"Santa is coming!"

Out in the woods
Santa picks up his big brown sack.

Slow Dog makes Mother Hen
a cup of tea.

He fills the chickens'
Christmas stockings.

He climbs up a ladder again
. . . and *climbs* down it.

Now it is late.
The moon shines down
and there are footprints
in the snow.

Slow Dog is fast asleep
and there are footprints
in the yard.

Mother Hen is fast asleep
and there are footprints
on the stairs.

The chickens
wake up.
They rub their little eyes.
"Who's this?"
White whiskers.
Red coat.
Black boots.
Brown sack.

"Santa is *here*!"

The chickens jump out of bed.
"Oh, Santa!"
They open their presents.
"Hooray!"
They climb on Santa's knee.

Oh no!
Those poor little chickens.
Who will save them?
What happens next?

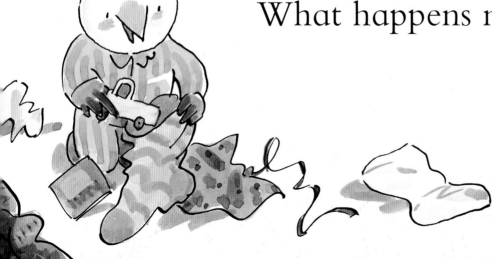

Downstairs
the clock strikes twelve.
Outside
the moon shines down.
Upstairs . . .
Santa plays with the chickens.

Yes – plays with them.
What else could he do?
After all . . .

It *is* Ch

ristmas!

The End

Now
turn
over

THE FAST FOX, SLOW DOG BOOKS

If you liked this story
and you're ready for another
Try

The Mother Hen Mysteries

In *The Mother Hen Mysteries*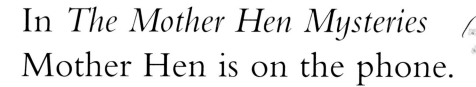
Mother Hen is on the phone.

Slow Dog is
on the bridge.

Fast Fox is on the prowl!

Oh no!
Those poor little
chickens . . .

. . . who can save them?